Dewey's Sheep Lose Sleep

(Or, How Mags Saved the Day)

By P. Bruce Uhrmacher & Cassie Trousas
Illustrated by Stephanie Schaefer

Orange Owl Publishing
Englewood, CO

For my family - past, present and future - P. B. U.

For Sofia, Ellena & Milt - my favorite stories of all - C. T.

To my family for always encouraging my doodles and tolerating
my aversion to growing up - S. S.

ISBN-13: 9780615960319
ISBN-10: 0615960316
Library of Congress Control Number: 2014902968

Printed by CreateSpace, An Amazon.com Company
Available from Amazon.com and other book stores

Please send all correspondence and letters to Mags to:
magsbooks4you@gmail.com

M onday began like any other day on Dewey Farm. Magdalena, whose friends call her Mags, woke up on her blue star blanket. She scratched behind her ears, cleaned her paws, and went to fetch her breakfast.

Then Mags set out to do her chores. She fed the ducks who were swimming laps on the pond and counted the chicks who were practicing the high jump. Then Mags went to check on the sheep.

The sheep were in a tizzy. Hal, who had a knack for reading clouds, had seen something unusual.

"I read the clouds closely," said Hal, "they say the Deweys are going to sell the farm." The sheep *baad* in great concern. The sheep loved Dewey Farm.

"Mr. Dewey had a bunch of coins in his hands and he was talking to another farmer," said Hal.

The sheep all *baad*. They walked in circles. They fell down and waved their legs in the air.

Some sheep were packing suitcases. Others were busy boarding up the windows of their houses. The sheep were upset and Mags was unsure what to do.

Mags ran over to the clever farm owls for advice.

"Look at this Mags," said Annie, "we're learning about the Olympic Games. Did you know that the first Olympics were played in Olympia, Greece? That's how they got their name."

"Great to know, but I have a problem to talk about," said Mags. Mags told the owls what Hal said.

"The Deweys would never sell the farm. Hal must be wrong," said Annie.

"There must be a way to help the sheep," Hoot said.

Mags stared at the owls while they crossed and uncrossed their wings.

"I got it!" Annie said. "A philosopher could do the trick."

"This book says a philosopher thinks big thoughts and asks big questions about everything in the world and more," said Annie, "but I wonder which one could help the sheep?"

"What about Socrates?" Hoot asked. "He was one of the greatest."

"Yes!" Annie said. "Socrates used philosophy to show people how to solve problems."

"Socrates lived a long, long time ago in Ancient Greece. It's been said that once Socrates stood in the town center for 24 hours just thinking," Hoot said.

"What if I could meet Socrates?" said Mags. "Wouldn't that be great?"

Hoot and Annie looked at each other and then at Mags.

"You can," said Annie, "you can use the wormhole. The wormhole is older than Dewey farm. Two worms, Luis and Clark, guard the magical wormhole. Whoever enters it can travel backward into history."

"Find Luis and Clark and tell them you need to go to Athens, Greece," said Hoot.

"Run!" said Annie.

Mags made a dash for the stable. Luis and Clark could hear Mags coming.

"*Hola* Mags," said Luis.

"Quick," said Mags. "Show me the wormhole. I need to go to Athens, Greece 450 B.C.E."

"Now that is a long time ago," Clark said. "Everyone in my family lives about 100 years. My great, great grandparents lived back then."

Moving the hay aside, the worms began to inch in and out of the mound of dirt creating a hole. The hole grew and grew and grew. Mags jumped in.

Mags' journey through the wormhole was like doing 103 log rolls.

The dog was tossed this way and that.

Mags popped out of the ground near an olive tree high on a hill. She looked around the beautiful city filled with white columns. In the distance lay the bright blue Aegean Sea.

     "I can see why a philosopher would want to live here," Mags whispered.

The dog trotted through town. The people of Athens spoke Greek, but Mags, being an animal, could understand all languages. After walking around for some time, Mags began to worry she would never find Socrates.

Then Mags saw people gathering in a large market. Curious, she ran over to see what was going on. Mags pushed through the crowd until she could see. What Mags saw was a young girl waving her arms.

"I just told my mom I won't gather olives anymore. It's dreadful," the girl said.

At that moment, a man interrupted the Athenian girl.

"Young girl, does your family rely on olives for food?" the man asked.

"Yes," she said.

"And does selling the olives give your family money?"

"Yes."

"Can your parents do all the work of gathering the olives themselves?"

"No."

"Do you see, then, that it is important for you to help your family?"

"Yes, Socrates."

Mags' ears pricked up. "It's Socrates!" she said. Mags jumped with excitement. Then all of the sudden she heard chirping sounds.

Looking down, Mags saw a grasshopper. One more jump and Mags might have squished it.

"Hey stranger," the grasshopper called out, "watch where you're jumping!"

"Sorry, I'm just so excited to have found Socrates," said Mags.

"Socrates! I come here often to listen to him," said the grasshopper.

"His Socratic dialogue is famous. It helped me solve many problems."

Mags shook to attention.

"That's why I'm here. I have a problem."

"There's a lot you can learn from Socrates," said the grasshopper and he leaped off into the crowd.

With no time to lose, Mags began her journey back to the wormhole.

All the way back she thought about Socrates, the young girl, and what the grasshopper said. Then, like thunder and lightening, she knew what had to be done.

"If I tell the sheep they are wrong about the clouds, they may not believe me," she thought aloud, "but if I ask them questions to show them the mistakes in their thinking, then they will see that the Deweys couldn't be selling the farm. Asking questions must be the Socratic dialogue."

Mags got so lost in her thoughts that she couldn't find the wormhole. Then at the top of the hill Mags spotted the olive tree. She began to climb. Panting and tired, Mags finally reached the tree and jumped into the wormhole.

Before long, Mags was tumbling and jumbling back through the wormhole and popped out of the ground with a poof near a haystack. Mags ran toward the sheep.

Rushing into the herd, Mags barked. The sheep stopped and stared at Mags.

"Let me ask you a question," Mags said to Hal, "what did you see in the clouds?"

"I saw a cloud in the shape of Mr. Dewey with a handful of coins," said Hal.

"How much money was there?" asked Mags.

"Well I couldn't exactly see," said Hal.

"Would you say there were fewer than 100 coins?" asked Mags.

"Yes," said another sheep. "Hal said that Mr. Dewey could hold them all in his two hands."

"Well then, even if each coin were a silver dollar, Mr. Dewey would have less than 100 dollars in his hands. Do you think Dewey Farm is worth more than 100 dollars?" Mags asked.

Hal and the sheep thought for a minute.

"I see my mistake," said Hal. The sheep all agreed that Mr. Dewey would never sell the farm for 100 dollars. Dewey Farm was worth much more than that. The sheep began to settle down and Mags sighed in relief.

Mags went to the owls' tree to tell them what she learned about Socrates.

"The Socratic dialogue really saved the day," Mags told the owls. Hoot listened to Mags' tale while Annie made notes in her book.

As Mags finished her story it was getting dark on Dewey Farm.

In the distance, Mags could hear a fuss among the sheep.

"It will just have to wait until tomorrow," whispered Mags, as she made her way home to curl up for the night on her blue star blanket.

THE END

OWLS' CORNER

Hoot and Annie discovered that the first Olympic Games were held in Olympia Greece. In fact, the first Olympic Games, then referred to as the Ancient Olympic Games, were first held in Olympia Greece in 776 B.C.E. The Olympics were stopped by the Romans in 394 A.D. but started again in 1896. Interestingly, in the beginning, the Olympics included events such as poetry and writing, in addition to the athletic events we see today.

Did you know?

Socrates often wore the same clothes to bed that he planned to wear the next day. He thought it was a waste of time to change clothes every day. What do you think?

GLOSSARY

Aegean Sea - An extension of the Mediterranean Sea between Greece and Turkey.

Athens - The capital of Greece located in the Eastern portion of the Greek mainland. Athens became the capital of Modern Greece in 1834.

Ancient Agora - In the story, Mags discovered Socrates in a large marketplace. In Socrates' time this area was known as the *Agora* meaning a large open place of gathering and civic assembly. Today this area is known as the *Ancient Agora* and is a popular tourist attraction in Athens, Greece.

Olympic Games - A series of international athletic contests held every four years. The games were first held in 776 B.C.E. as a festival of athletic games and contests of choral poetry and dance.

The five-ringed symbol shown here was designed in 1912 and is the international symbol and trademark of the modern Olympic Movement.

Philosopher - One who lives and and thinks according to a particular set of ideas.

Socrates (470?-399 B.C.E.) - A Greek Philosopher who initiated a question-answer method of teaching as a means of achieving knowledge.

Socratic Method (dialogue) - A technique of teaching or discussion used by Socrates involving the asking of a series of questions that lead the answerer to a logical conclusion.

ABOUT THE AUTHORS

Bruce Uhrmacher lives in Denver, Colorado. With his wife Lisa and their kids, Arianna, Paul, and by choice and with full knowledge, Stephanie; Bruce had the privilege of being taught by a progression of dog educators: Maggie, Frankie, and Allie (all of whom in personality, breed and general determination were the combined inspiration for Mags). Also to be thanked are Izzi, Tessa, Akayla and not to be forgotten: Skippy, Banjo, Butch and the one feline in the mix, Moonbeam.

Cassie Trousas lives in Northern Virginia with her Greek-born husband, Miltos and two daughters, Sofia and Ellena. She lived in Greece for one year on the Ionian island of Corfu. Cassie and her family have been to Athens many times and have visited many of the sites seen by Mags in the story. Cassie's dog, a Tibetan Spaniel named Kasmil, was also born in Greece and traveled to the United States to be with her new family, although Kasmil traveled by plane rather than wormhole.

Stephanie Schaefer holds a degree in Art History & Studio Art from The University of Colorado. Stephanie loves the outdoors and spends much of her time rafting, rock climbing, hiking, camping, and snowboarding with her dogs Akela and Ollie. She has also been blessed with a family (by birth and by choice) who encourage her creativity. Stephanie found inspiration for Mags in the Uhrmacher's family dog, Frankie. Frankie had one of the most perceptive gazes Stephanie has ever encountered in a dog.

BLANK

www.ingramcontent.com/pod-product-compliance
Lightning Source LLC
Chambersburg PA
CBHW041607120626
46551CB00002B/340